Margaret's Magical Crown

A Day at The County Fair

by Pamela Allegrezza

Illustrations by Blueberry Illustrations

ISBN-13:978-1511935067

ISBN-10:1511935065

Margaret is a little girl who moves into a big old house. While exploring her new house, she finds a library with many books, but the books are not the most fascinating thing she discovers. She discovers a magical golden crown. The crown has a green emerald and the letters "JB" on it. Margaret soon learns the letters "JB" stand for Jelly Bean, a new found friend who can fit in her pocket or ride on her shoulder. When Margaret wears the crown and reads a book, she is spun into the story.

Up until now, Margaret's life has been uneventful, but this lovable pair becomes best friends. This is a story of friendship and imagination. Come along with Margaret and Jelly Bean and share in their world of magical adventures.

One rainy day Margaret explores her library
looking for a fun book to read.
She sees a book with a colorful cover called
A Day At The County Fair.
Then, out of the corner of her eye,
she sees a golden crown with
a green emerald and the letters "JB."

Margaret sits down quietly in her library with
the book and the golden crown.
She carefully puts the crown on her head.
It fits perfectly! Feeling like a princess, Margaret
begins to read and the crown begins to spin.
Then, to her surprise, she hears herself saying....

Whoaa...Whoaa...
"Margaret shrieks, where am I?"
"You are on Sassy Sue in the starting
gate of the race."
"What race, asks Margaret" in a surprised voice.
"Why, the horse race at the county
fair of course", a little voice replies.
Oh my "who are you asks Margaret?"
The little voice replies, "my name is Jelly Bean."
"I'm your friend and I'll be with you in all
of your adventures."

Margaret suddenly hears, And they're off!
Out of the gate as fast as lightening
they race down the track.
"Oh my, we're moving so fast, I'm frightened",
cries Margaret. "Hold on tight Margaret,
Sassy Sue is a good horse and
she will take good care of us", replies Jelly Bean.

Faster and faster Sassy Sue races
around the track.
Around the curve passing Silly Billy.
They're racing full speed ahead, but Sassy Sue
streaks by like a flash of light.

Down the stretch they race passing Frilly Lilly.
Frilly Lilly is no match for Sassy Sue.
"Wow, look at Sassy Sue run! She is going to
win the blue ribbon for sure," says Frilly Lilly.
Like a whirlwind Sassy Sue is out of site.

Margaret becomes so excited with
the cheering of the crowd.
Her heart begins to beat faster and
faster with every gallop as they
reach the finish line.
The wind blowing in her face,
Margaret shouts out, "I'm flying, I'm flying."
Jelly Bean shouts out, "Go Sassy Sue, Go!"

Across the finish line at the speed
of light they go!
"Oh we won, we won," says Margaret.
She giggles as they wave to
the cheering crowd.
"That race was so much fun!"

The End

Margaret and Jelly Bean have many
magical adventures together.
Their day at the county fair is now over.
What will be their next fun adventure?

Margaret and Jelly Bean are presented
with the blue ribbon and a gold trophy.
Sassy Sue stands proud as she is
presented with a delicious red apple.
Margaret is so happy she has a new friend to
share in her fun-filled magical adventures.
Then with the click of the photographer's
camera her crown begins to spin and it's
off to the next big adventure.

Made in the USA
Charleston, SC
29 May 2015